THE LETTERS OF MAGDALEN MONTAGUE

THE LETTERS OF MAGDALEN MONTAGUE

a novella by

ELEANOR BOURG NICHOLSON

CHRISM
PRESS

This is a work of fiction. All characters and events portrayed in this novel are either fictitious or used fictitiously.

THE LETTERS OF MAGDALEN MONTAGUE

Chrism Press, a division of WhiteFire Publishing
13607 Bedford Rd NE
Cumberland, MD 21502

ISBN: 978-1-941720-50-9 (print)
978-1-941720-51-6 (digital)

Previously published by Kaufmann Publishing, copyright © 2011.
Originally published in serial form in *Dappled Things* Magazine, 2007-2008.

CONTENTS

CONTENTS

To J.

Yrs. affectly, etc.

—R

PROLOGUE

On 4 April 1947, a house on the Rue des Trois Frères, raided by the Nazis and left untenanted since the liberation of Paris, was sold. Records of past ownership had been destroyed during the occupation, and, as memory is short in that district, little was known of the man who had most recently lived there. No stories were known to explain his departure. How could there be, at a time when so many were dead or disappeared without a trace? He might have evacuated the city with so many others; he might have been imprisoned; he might have been dead.

In the far corner of a dark and cluttered attic, a large, flat-topped trunk of soiled gray Trianon canvas was found. A label inside the lid boldly proclaimed the craftsmanship of Louis Vuitton, *Malletier à Paris.* Collaborator.

The trunk contained an eclectic collection of objects, like those found in most deserted houses—the *disjecta membra* of a life. Old clothes of a faded, though still gaudy, flavor. Five packets of letters. A crate of particularly colorful erotica. The manuscript of a rather sordid novel. And, at the bottom, a dusty, soiled holy card with tinny gilt edging to frame a cheerful, young martyr attired in doublet, hose, and a ruff who leaned upon the rack beside him as if it were the pleasantest deathbed ever known to man. The card commemorated a young man's ordination to the priesthood, dated 1915. The priest's name was so faded as to be entirely illegible.

These are the letters.

I: THE CHARACTER OF MAGDALEN MONTAGUE

3 MARCH 1902
LONDON

MY DEAR R.,

The character of Magdalen Montague has long been considered an acceptable topic of public discourse, so I feel utterly justified in writing to you about it. The subject has, in fact, proved to be an invaluable stimulus to waning conversations. One only has to reference that sublimely intriguing yet eminently respectable personage, and interest is revived, animation awakened. I witnessed a singular demonstration of this phenomena the other day when I had the misfortune to meet that Medusa's head borne on a sea of bombazine—Lady Fleming, you know. I had no idea that park lanes so readily afforded corners until I was backed into one by her formidable ugliness and assailed with political pamphlets and moral lessons.

“Young man,” she said, in that particularly nasal tone of hers, “I want to have a talk with you…”

Just as she was on the brink of indicting me for the suffering of the poverty-stricken masses, I parried the thrust and inquired, “And what do you think of Magdalen Montague?”

The effect was instantaneous.

“Miss Montague!” And then, surpassing my wildest expectations, she sneered. It was like a moment in a frightfully bad play—one of those abhorrent things that occasionally blights Leicester Square. Reviled by those with taste, these monstrosities are invariably guaranteed a two-year run. As I have already noted, the mention of Magdalen Montague produces a similar effect. It stimulates conversation, provokes passionate opinions, and thus must be revered as an inexhaustible source of social dynamite. This is especially true with recent events to reintensify opinions and passions and reawaken general interest.

Of course, you can hardly be expected to know the recent Montague saga. Their house is closed. Montague, his wife, and the noxious child have fled to some stagnant watering place. They left only three days ago, the day after a dinner party in their house. (That was the night of that sordid affair of Henry Godwin’s.) The reasons for Montague’s self-imposed exile are unknown, although the hypotheses born of the minds of gossipers are legion. And Magdalen Montague is gone…perhaps forever.

I never knew the first Mrs. Montague, and it is quite unlikely that you did either. I believe she died at the birth of the formidable Magdalen; and indeed the birthing of that being might well have proved deadly to a weak maternal vessel. Yet she must have been a remarkable woman. Quite unlike her recent replacement—that light, bright, gentle ornament bears about in her head only as much in brains as might be considered absolutely necessary for existence. She and her stepdaughter are the most incongruous pair, with Magdalen towering above the light little coquette in stature and age. She must be at least ten years older in reality and at least three centuries older in terms of soul. What can have possessed Montague to marry the little blonde sprite?

I do not consider these questions because of recent events. As a matter of fact, I have for some time been occupied in contemplating the many problems inherent in Magdalen Montague. Before I can fully describe recent events, I feel that I owe it to myself to describe the circumstances of that early contemplation. Otherwise, you will not be able to understand why I have for so long and so seriously been fascinated by this strange topic.

I had not seen Magdalen Montague in years. When Montague married his second wife so long after the death of his first, the family spent a great deal of time in the country. Someplace up north where lack of style and lack of warmth compete to stupefy the brain.

I heard that the lassie wife had birthed a whimpering babe, presenting her mustachioed lord with another female encumbrance. I met said wife and babe (now a frilled and frocked young suburban denizen of three or four years old) walking in the park at the start of the season. Montague looked, as always, like a colonel who has absentmindedly misplaced India. The wife simpered and caressed the babe. The babe hid in the simpering wife's skirts. Little wonder that I fled the scene as quickly as possible. I spared only a passing thought for the mysterious, absent figure of Magdalen Montague.

About a fortnight ago I was wandering around South Kensington and meandered my way up Cromwell Road. I found myself standing outside that monstrous hulk of a church deposited on London by Newman or some other tiresome priest during the last twenty or so years. The doors stood open and a milling crowd of dupes were spilling out into the street, impeding the progress of innocent passersby like myself. I was just composing several choice and mocking phrases to be muttered in debonair asides into the sympathetic ears of London during future parties when my attention was diverted by an extraordinary sight. Magdalen Montague was standing on the steps of the blighted oratory. She was even shaking hands with the lace-encumbered priest. This extraordinary woman stood calmly, even contentedly, amid the most pathetic and gullible crowd I had witnessed that morning.

I know that you have seen Magdalen Montague many times and do not describe her for your benefit. Indeed, her physical appearance could be briefly sketched—tall, large-boned, and dark-featured, she is an imposing figure and not at all a pretty one. Magdalen Montague is no beauty. Her features are far too unorthodox. But she is striking. The eyes are large, dark, and keen, set off to great advantage by a pair of heavy, dark eyebrows. The mouth is too wide to be truly feminine, but it seethes with power and unawakened passion. In fact, she is like a magnificent sculpture of a darkened Athena—militant, wise, and impenetrable. One can only dream of what she must have been in her childhood. She is not feminine, yet I have the distinct suspicion that she was born more truly a woman than the most certifiably female matron.

She has not the face that launched a thousand ships, but had she a mind to do so, Magdalen Montague might engulf three Troys in an apocalyptic conflagration. That quiet, controlled countenance screams tempest, trauma, terror, and passion. The negligible observer will not note it. He will pass this supernatural being in the street and marvel not. But he who can capture that eye and provoke the flame of self-expression therein might count himself a greater artisan than Pygmalion.

I bid her good morning. "You have been to church," I noted.

She did not smile, but her air was not unfriendly. "Yes."

"You are quite a devotee of despised Popery?"

Her eyes remained unreadable. "And you are a devotee of despised ennui."

I shrugged. "I have no need for father confessors or Puritan lectures. Religion is only a waste of time. And time, which is always a bore anyway, must be filled with more distracting pleasures than incense and grubby beads can provide."

She did not reply. If I had expected an argument, I was disappointed. She did not even look distressed. She merely glanced into my face, wished me a pleasant good morning, and strode away up the street.

Why did she reject this fine opportunity for sophisticated confabulation? We might have lapsed into witty wordplay, each probing into the other rich, resistant soul standing on the churchly stair. We might have plumbed the depths of human existence, shocked the lazy Popish birds from their roosts amongst the cluttering statuary. We might have shaken the cheerful countenance of that vestment-laden Jesuit who returned undeterred into the church, no doubt thinking more of a waiting supper than any pedestrian mysticism.

I stood for a moment, uncertain what to do. It is, of course, against my principles to venture into places of the so-called "sacred," but principles were made to be broken, and such a study as the character of Magdalen Montague provides demands extraordinary measures. All visible ranks of Popery had departed. I was alone beside the church. I flicked an invisible speck of dust from my impeccable jacket sleeve, hauled open the massive door, and walked in.

What did I find, my friend? I am no Ruskin acolyte to be drawn into the pretense of divine contemplation by manmade beauty. I saw a dark, dank, candle-infested vault. Have you ever wandered into one of these icon-ridden monstrosities? Imaginative decorations born of a mercifully forsaken aesthetic crowd every corner. The very dust seems oppressed with the stench of fetid incense. Intense, nauseating, suffocating. As if they wanted to stifle unsuspecting victims into submissive, mewling adoration. So dark and so full of heavy silence.

I looked about, shuddered, and moved further up the aisle toward a gleam of cleansing sunlight. I have always appreciated atmosphere, as you know, and have been known to ridicule gothic melodrama with considerable wit and vivacity; but I don't mind confessing that the filthy church filled me with disgust, horror, and a queasy nervousness beyond expectation. Nothing but the most intense attraction could keep me in that moribund place. Even so, as I stood there shivering, my curiosity intensified. What could bring that astonishing being, that goddess, into this empty place? There must be a reason. It cannot be mere superstition that draws her.

I remembered then that the first Lady Montague had been of an ancient family. One of those primordial recusant lines who would have rushed into Tyburn and gloried in suicidal fanaticism. Bane of the stalwart

Church of England and object of intense disgust to modern intellects. I believe Montague is thoroughly high church, inasmuch as he considers religion at all. And I can hardly imagine his present Domina chanting *aves* and inhaling incense. It is possible that the motherless girl—if Magdalen was ever so commonplace a thing as a girl—was raised according to the bizarre tenets of her mater's Romish religion. But the enigmatic young Montague cannot be of that ilk. Her namesake the viscountess was, by report, of formidable stature; let us imagine that she who braved the displeasure of Good Queen Bess is reincarnated and returns to Popery. Satisfying as that theory might be, there must be a different reason, a different motivation for her visits to this tawdry haven of forgotten ritual.

Can there be some man who frequents the Church? I had not noticed the departing worshippers. I had assumed them uninteresting and unpleasing. But perhaps there was some man in the crowd. He would have to be an extraordinary man to stir the passions of that dark goddess. A grungy, earthy laborer? A cold ascetic? An oily foreigner? What sort of man must he be? Perhaps they left squalid love letters in the crevices behind that abhorrent statue—one can only suppose it is meant to be some sycophantic female saint. There can be no other explanation for the insipid expression plastered on her face.

I was just about to glance behind the statue, in the nervous hope of finding something as boring and sordid as a written confession of repressed sexual excitement, when a hand touched my shoulder. I wheeled around, almost expecting to face the imagined lover. It was merely the priest. How silently the man creeps up on one!

"Can I help you, my son?" he asked with what I suppose was meant to be kindness but struck me as mere pandering.

"No." I was surprised at the loudness of my voice. I cleared my throat and began again, "No...Thank you, Father."

"You are not, I think, a Catholic..."

"No." Again, the abruptness of my reply annoyed me. Why was I behaving like a sullen child caught in some unseemly act? It must be the effect that eerie Jesuit has on those not deceived by his priestcraft.

"You have come to study some of our artwork, perhaps?"

"No, I...was merely curious. I am sorry if I have given offense." My tone had become sneering. Would the besotted little acolyte chase me from his beloved mausoleum?

"Don't apologize. We welcome any respectful adorer."

And with that contentious remark and a meek little bow, he scurried off, the black dress in which he was ensconced flowing around his ankles. How can that noisy, noisome little man have crept so undetected to my side?

The meeting dispelled any further daring from my soul. I could not rest until I was free of that strange place with its gaudy trappings and archaic atmosphere. I left the church and walked away, drinking in the dull light and odorous liberty of a London street.

You must pardon me, my friend, if I indulge these descriptive whims. I have often wondered at the unrealistic dedication of the heroine of an epistolary novel who records conversations of immeasurable length without considering the patience or sanity of her readers. But if the feverish fascination that drives me also motivates the insipid young lady whose adventures in Brighton fill three volumes, I can never sneer at Evelina more.

I did not see Magdalen Montague again for more than a week, taking good care in that time to avoid the taint of further association with nauseating religiosity. Then, only a few days ago, I received an invitation to an evening party at the Montagues. At moments such as the present, the height of the London season, they dabble in society. The second Mrs. Montague has not the brains to support anything more than dabbling, her aged husband is too easily bored, and one can only suppose that the inscrutable Magdalen is too unearthly a being to take much pleasure in frivolity and small talk. She could not support small talk. The opportunity afforded by such an invitation, therefore, was not to be missed.

Accordingly, I found myself two evenings ago in the superficially stylish drawing room of young Mrs. Montague, smiling at that lady's obnoxious tittering while glancing toward the door, awaiting her stepdaughter's entrance. How would the woman attire herself for the evening? A bold red? A sober black? A stunning pastel that would shock the company by clashing with her dark complexion?

The door opened and Magdalen stood before us, graceful in cold purple silk. I noted with approbation the absence of gloves. Those large, powerful, beautiful hands should never be concealed at an evening party. Admiration held me back a moment too long, and her attention was claimed by that doddering Lord Ingleton. He drooled in her face for a few moments. Was she impatient to flee his abhorrent dullness? If so, she made no move to escape, even when opportunities for flight abounded. He moved away, smiling at something she had murmured, but before I could step in and demand her attention, a flurry of matronly skirts announced conquest by one or another unattractive gorgon of advanced years.

It was some minutes before I could insinuate myself into her path.

"Good evening, Miss Montague," I said with my most charming smile. She acknowledged my greeting with a brief smile in return. How magnificently that woman's face is sculptured.

I complimented her on the fine gathering of bright lights and dim minds. She nodded.

"I glanced inside your church on Cromwell Street the other day after we met."

"Indeed?"

"An interesting building."

She did not reply. She did not even nod her head. She merely looked.

"And I believe I met your resident priest."

Again, there was no reply. I decided to change my line of attack. Magdalen Montague, you might or might not know, is said to dote on her diminutive stepsister. A ringletted blonde with her mother's dimples and a merry laugh, she skips in the park, speaks charmingly to guests, and bores me to tears with her trite prattle.

"And the dear little Miss Montague," I said coyly, "are we not to be graced by her presence?"

Only a fool would expect to win over the confidence of Magdalen Montague with idle flattery, but if softening is possible for a myth in the flesh, she did so then. "Bella is asleep."

"What a pity!" I began, but catching her penetrating eye, I stopped. An overabundance of enthusiasm for the detested child could not hope to be believed. "You are fond of the child?"

"Yes."

"It must be a different house for you now."

"Yes." There was no bitterness, no distress. I was wrong when I said Magdalen Montague could not support small talk. She was born to crush small talk utterly.

"Will there be music this evening?"

"Yes, I believe Mrs. Montague intends to grace us with a performance."

"And you?"

"I am not averse to playing, although I do not enjoy performing."

That was something. The expression of personality relies on negation.

"Why do you dislike performing?"

"Perhaps it is from lack of study."

That was an unfair avoidance of the question. I pressed further. "But I have been told that you are an impressive musician."

"By whom?"

Devil take the woman. She absolutely refused to accept an innocuous compliment.

"Oh, I believe it is generally known. But you are inclined to think your education insufficient?"

"No, I said perhaps that is why I dislike performing."

We had reached an impasse. Well, another impasse. I bowed. She bowed. I moved across the room. Why did I fall back so easily from her implacable defenses? You well may wonder. But I had not fled the battle. I'd merely postponed my attack. I was determined to lay siege to the lime-tree bower prison of her mind. If she was reluctant to perform, I would be the hand that drew or dragged her to the instrument.

In theory, I was prepared to beg, beseech, implore, or demand. In fact, it required little more than a quiet insinuation to simple Mrs. Montague that a performance by her stepdaughter would give great pleasure to the assembled throng. A bright-eyed request was made and the Magdalen acquiesced.

It was, of course, an astonishing performance. I had hoped to provoke her into self-expression, and the room was rife with it, but I did not think myself victorious. I cannot recall what she played. Beethoven, Mozart, Chopin, or any of half-a-dozen accepted composers. Her execution was faultless, and the passion well-articulated and stirring. And it was effortless. One expected her life's blood to spill out over the keys, a being expended in an overflow of musical greatness. But the Magdalen Montague who began was the Magdalen Montague who concluded. Quiet. Composed. Unreadable.

Such a performance could not help but stun the audience into silence. Perhaps they were too stupid to appreciate the superiority of her talent. In that brief moment, before the need for applause could be satisfied or the mind could move to signal applause to ready hands, a blood-curdling scream rent the silence.

I don't suppose I had ever heard a "blood-curdling scream"—it is the sort of thing one reads of in gothic novels and does not experience in the everyday. This shrill cry—almost animalistic in its pure, unadulterated terror—sent a shock through the company. Surprise, coming so quickly on the heels of the overwhelming sensual intoxication of the song brought general impotence. Each man stared wide-eyed at his fellow, and the women sat in a sort of frozen hysteria. No one moved. No one. Except Magdalen Montague.

At the moment the scream pierced the solemn stillness, she rose from her place at the piano and fled from the room, vanishing from our sight with the rapidity of a spectre. I could not hear her foot on the stair; perhaps she flew beyond every obstacle, like Demeter racing to rescue the weeping Persephone from the jaws of lecherous Hades.

Then movement was again afforded us, and militant Montague ran from the room after his daughter. We followed in a bedraggled mess of confused intentions and fears. No man stayed to comfort the frantic nerves of the little mother.

At the foot of the stairs I paused and looked up. Montague had passed the landing and stood looking up at the goddess. A weeping mass of curls and lacy nightdress was huddled in her arms.

"Lina! Lina!" wept the child, clinging to that powerful neck. The whole situation had melted into the dullness of melodrama. A child's pathetic nightmare, not an epic crisis, had disturbed the evening. I gazed with aversion at the perpetrator of this distasteful anticlimax. I was overwhelmed with a desire to strike the tawdry infant into silence and pry her arms from about the Magdalen.

From thence the dinner party lapsed into mundane and predictable dullness. The Magdalen disappeared upstairs and did not return. The little mother was too nervous to fulfill her obligations as hostess and instead graced us with many reiterated expressions of distress, concern, and overall nervousness. Matrons aplenty clustered round her, offering advice, encouraging the tragicomedy. Montague looked blank and talked of indifferent subjects to anyone who would listen. I left the house the moment retreat was made possible. I might have constructed an excuse for departure earlier but waited in vain to see if the unfathomable Magdalen would reappear.

THE NEXT MORNING WE ALL AWOKE TO THE SENSATIONAL news of Henry Godwin's death. You know his mad wife has been a nuisance for years upon years? Well, it seems he inclined toward intoxicated violence and exacted a heavy fine for her mindless dependence. The servants have industriously circulated a most repulsive tale of insanity and murder that I will (without vouching for its truthfulness) give you.

That night, the very night of the party, Godwin set about the madwoman with particular ferocity and left her huddled and weeping somewhere in the house. The maid claims her mistress was ravaged and beaten in her boudoir, left in less than her shift.

The butler insists it was the drawing room and that innumerable family treasures were destroyed in the wake of Godwin's vicious fury. (As the family was only modestly outfitted, it is difficult to imagine mounds of crystal shattered against priceless paintings, but I give you the fellow's story to counterbalance the maid's rape of Lucrece.) The cook makes no comment, and the scullery maid does nothing but cry. Godwin left his beloved spouse, they all agree, and went to drink his way to further villainy.

The wife crept to his side while he snored in intoxicated slumber and plunged a large hatpin into his heart and brain a dozen or so times. Would a hatpin survive this harrowing experience? Owing to my limited experience of such matters, I cannot say. I merely give you the story as it is popularly told.

She then beat his bleeding corpse with whatever came to hand—a bloody and ineffectual pillow, says the maid; a broken bottle, says the butler. The cook makes no comment, and the scullery maid does nothing but cry.

I ought to apologize to you for recounting such a sensational tale, but really it strikes me that everyday melodrama is not half as entertaining as the saga of the Montague woman as I see it. Although by itself the sordid affair provides little stimulus for the mind, its aftermath is full of perplexing interest. That was three days ago. And that same day the Montague household, just across the street from the torrid murder scene, was closed up. The family is gone, supposedly to Bath or the like. Is this the reason for the child's ill-timed nightmare? Did the mewling infant wake and witness some dark deed by moonlight?

And what of the Magdalen? Is she dead in a ditch? Has she eloped with some unknown lover? Has she been sent to the country in disgrace? Can it be that she carried on a sordid affair with the villainous Godwin? Does she now despair at his death?

I have wandered the streets for hours, passing her strange oratory again and again. I even ventured inside once but found nothing beyond my own disgust. Where can she be? Why is she not with her aged father, simple stepmother, and the noxious babe?

Well, my friend, I have written you an appallingly lengthy missive, but I do hope you will pardon me. Perhaps it is the uncharacteristic dullness of London that inspired me to such loquacity. But I think not. How could one write less with such a fascinating subject as the character of Magdalen Montague? I can only hope that the tale will unfold with appropriate drama to justify the composition of a second installment.

Until then, I remain

Yrs, etc.

THE MORNING IS DAWNING. I HAVE NOT SLEPT. I cannot sleep. My dear fellow, I can hardly write to tell you. I am so astonished. The news that has come. I don't know why it has so unsettled me. Why should it be so extraordinary? Why so startling? Is it drama or is it farce?

Magdalen Montague is in a convent at Tyburn.

Why? Why has she done this? What can have motivated her? Has the stifling, noxious spell of that squalid oratory infiltrated her mind? Has she rushed from the failure of seamy sensual pleasure into that haven of despair and impotence? Has she...Is there...

I am... I must go outside for a time. The light is still dim, and the streets are rank with the fetid smog of early morning. But I must go out. How strange the world appears this morning.

—J.

II: THE FLIGHT FROM MAGDALEN MONTAGUE

2 April 1902
Budapest

My dear R.,

You well may wonder at my address! Especially since my last missive (which was of appalling length, I know) was sent to you from the fetid bosom of our revered island. Yes, my friend, I have fled sodden London and become, for the sake of my health, a temporary expatriate. I find the rest of the world as tedious as London can ever be, in season or out. I am not surprised. The world has been dull for as long as I have known it, and I am not so arrogant as to suppose that it was not dull before I graced it with my presence.

"How goes your time abroad?" That is the established question, and therefore you must ask it. I answer, "It is dull." "How do you like Budapest?" That is your next question. We shall obey the laws of polite society, not out of respect or devotion to their arbitrary rule but because there are no original remarks left to us. I reply, "I do not like it." "How long shall you be away?" Perhaps you may proffer this question next, as it is quite respectable and used in the best houses. "Forever," is my response, "or, at least, until such time as I waste away from boredom."

The city is dirty, the natives primitive, and the society nauseous. There is an English community, of course, and they might have been imported from one of our drawing rooms. Big-bosomed, antique matrons with pale moustaches; timid, rabbit-brained daughters with no bosoms at all; manly sons with so much muscle that it takes up the cranial space usually allotted to brains; and ancient patriarchs who have been talking of the same things since the world began, who rely upon fashion to dictate their opinions. In sum, a tourist's sample of the landed gentry, their tenacity of life and inability to live it. Immortal fathers who drag on their existences for the sole purpose of watching their sons suffer in penury. An age-old story, and one I know from experience.

Even scandal has lost its power to entertain. Murder and mayhem could not rouse interest in this jaded mind. A full-scale revolution might be the solution, especially if it brought motiveless and merciless violence. If a few of those matrons and their opinionated patriarchs were put to the sword, it might give us something interesting to look at in the streets. But who could have the energy to promote such an agenda? I am sure I do not. There are no men of spirit or soul amongst us anymore.

There is, of course, one advantage that Budapest can always boast over London. The city is refreshingly lacking in Magdalen Montagues. Yes, indeed, I flee my strange illness after the defection of that fascinating character, that woman who gathered an ocean of artistic potential and squirreled it away to sacrilegious squander in a living tomb of virginal stagnancy. But enough of the lost Magdalen. I have come to recover from her descent into soulless mediocrity.

"Why did I not come to you in Paris?" That will be your next question, and I don't quite know how to answer it. Perhaps I am enjoying the melodrama of the present moment—wandering in miserable self-exile, the weary intellect pines for the woman he did not possess. Your recent letter scoffed at the purported power of MM. I expected it and valued the composing power of your scorn. Melodrama cannot touch, nor Papist incantations waver, your self-possessed disgust. You have always maintained contemptuous tranquility better than I.

As for this traveling—well, at least it is something to do. I know you do not wonder at my world-weary indecision. It was you who first instructed me in the delights and the dullness of this aesthete existence.

Oh, I have not mentioned the boy. There has been one rather interesting meeting, one glimmer in this bleak sojourn. My hotel (with its amenities most foul) employs a seedy group of profligates—cleaning women who look as if they have never bothered to clean themselves, waiters who reek of the unswept streets, and a host of brainless young men so pock-faced as to startle the guests and make them appreciate the squalor of their surroundings in contrast. Among this horde of purposeless young dogs, there is one particularly repulsive young man who may have a spark of divine fire nestled behind his unprepossessing visage. He is so ugly his face is almost beautiful—high cheekbones; a lean face; large, luminous, leering eyes; an abnormally large and flat nose; a wide, lipless mouth; and a bony, pointy chin. His name is Domokos Juhász, and he is an orphan (or says he is). The incestuous progeny of Satan and his daughter Sin? He certainly looks the part.

Do not suppose I have any particular design on the boy. You know I have never inclined toward your favored breed of indulgence. I do not object to it, but neither am I drawn to it. Do as you will, as I know you certainly shall. But I am tempted to interest myself in young Domokos Juhász. His English is as broken as his crooked, blackened teeth, and when he speaks it seems as if the potential for exquisitely ugly blasphemy hovers all around us.

Each morning he greets me the same way.

"*Jó reggelt, angolman*," he says to me in his broken English, "You go far today, *igen*?"

"All the way to nowhere," I respond.

He laughs through those teeth of his, and I suspect him of malevolence. "Yes, yes, Nowhere. Is a far place to go."

Shall I corrupt him? He looks eminently corruptible. Shall I play Des Esseintes and instruct this youth in the arts of decadence? I fear not. Such an endeavor would require more energy than I have at present. But I mark him and find him curious. A budding young emissary for the demoniac sublime? Was not Satan himself captivating in all of his hideousness?

All of this musing means little, of course. Tonight I am to be amused by company! I shall not stand it long. When oblivion appears less tedious than this torpid reality, I shall take advantage of some fine and delicate potions I have with me. This is not compulsive melodrama; you know I am too world-weary to bother with petty addiction. The only solace this world can afford to us suffering intellects is an opportunity to escape it.

With an arrogant sneer becoming to one of my temperament and your tutelage,

Yrs, etc.

Postscript: Give my questionable love to S. or M. or whatever the names of your current assemblage may be. I am sure that Budapest will soon grow stale, and I shall be with you again in your reveling throng of dullards. This time we must avoid the Rue M., for there can be no necessity for any sort of repetition that might seem to demonstrate a monogamic trend.

---

3 April 1902
Budapest

R.,

I must write. I must tell you. I must tell someone. If I do not order this tumult in my brain, I shall truly run mad. I am confused. These sensations are like the abject terror and bewilderment of inarticulate childhood, but I am no child.

I know you are amazed. Perhaps I do truly run mad. In any case, it should prove an interesting study. And entertaining. I should be heartily entertained. I am not. You must find entertainment, then.

I shall start at the beginning, if there is one. Shall you like the role of a father confessor? Laugh, my friend, and I shall try to laugh with you. Melodrama will cause you no disquiet. And your composure shall serve mine, as it so often has.

The evening was young and I was on my way to boredom and thinking of soothing nothingness, of drowning in Lethean stupor. Perverse fancy took me. I would walk. It seemed I was of a mind to drift amongst the ebb and flow, the bustle, the fleeting and the infinite (as it has been said). I tried to rouse myself to become the quintessential man of the crowd, but disgust disarmed the impulse to marvel at the spectacle of men, and I desired nothing more than to be aloof from the petty horde while in its midst. I made my way through the city, wandering and watching the people—fat, ugly women and stupid, brutish men. All hustling and bustling as if existence were of significance. A pageant of pathetic mediocrity. If I could but awaken sufficient interest and energy, I might really be brought to despair of mankind.

I had passed the palace—like most, a smorgasbord of uninspired artistic ambitions—and I must have walked quite a way, for I found myself in a square with the ostentatious Mátyás Templom before me. This gargantuan Papist thing is, I am told, associated with their Madonna. Politics will always win over sentimentality and superstition—the church is known by the name of King someone-or-other who threw forints at the construction. I ignored the church. I deserted the comfort of a London season for this desert just so I might be spared the unsettling effect of Popery. Yes, it is unsettling. It must be that which so disturbs me. Even you must admit that there is something behind all of this.

But I was describing the square. In keeping with the pretentious, gaudy grandeur of the place, there is an opulent column in the square—a groveling tribute to a Papist triune God, constructed after a plague or a war or some such business. How apt the poor are to waste their gratitude on tawdry edifices they haven't the wits to disdain. I disregarded the column altogether and went to admire the statue of Pallas Athena, which stands in one corner of the square. My attention could not remain there long. The goddess reminded me uncomfortably of the lost Magdalen.

I thought of Domokos Juhász and wondered if I should forego the planned evening in favor of leading that willing young sinner astray. It could prove interesting. Perhaps the role of Des Esseintes attracted me after all.

I found myself walking toward the monstrosity. What drew me? I did not and even now do not know. Startled and uneasy, I drew myself up and halted, irresolute, on the doorstep before the ornate door. A strange piece of work. Hideous yet somehow wonderful. Like the leering Domokos.

Would I be frightened away by the sacred dust of theatrical priestcraft? My reason rebelled against the uncertainty or timidity of my stomach. Against my very will, with Pallas and Domokos almost forgotten, I opened the door and passed inside.

Can you feel the turmoil of the ages? Can you stand on the steps of a building and tremble at the rush of history? As I stood there, I could hear the footsteps of a legion of pilgrims. Mindless sheep herding eagerly into the sullen darkness. The clash of battle I heard too and felt the Turkish dishonor as fresh as if they stood there before me, championing this strange space, this weighty darkness, for Mohammed. Rape, horror, death, and despair. And something else. Something strange and oppressive. Is it that which they call peace? I call it hell. An inferno of unreal atmosphere.

What was it that unsettled me so? I do not know. Yet I think it was that sameness of the place that unnerved me. So far from the hideous, heavy silence of the oratory in which I once stood, moments after leaving the Montague, yet so like it. Could she be outside waiting for me?

I walked away from her ghost and was lost in the flickering darkness of the empty church. I wandered into the medieval crypt and glanced into a highly decorated chapel dedicated to some timid boy martyr. All about me was darkness and that oppressive silence. I wandered in and about the arches and columns, through stark wooden benches where the credulous crowd congregates, glancing at artistic displays barely perceptible through the gloom.

The sacred box was there. The tabernacle. The Ark of the Covenant. The gaudy idol of the ignorant poor and the weapon of deluded princes. As I stood there, a feeling of *Gesamtkunstwerk* overwhelmed me. As if I had stumbled upon an absolute synthesis I could not understand. It horrified me. I looked upon the strange, hideous prison, sick at the thought of what was contained inside it. Morbid Papists claim it holds the divine physical. I know it to be worthless bread. But what if the doors were to open, drawn by the hand of the Magdalen, and the bloody limbs of the crucified were displayed? What if the sound in my ears was not the throbbing of my heart but that of his?

I closed my eyes, but still I saw it. I stood as if I had been turned to stone, trembling in the darkness of my closed eyes, powerless in the grasp of that basilisk vision. A strange, conflicted, trampled, bleeding mass. A bloody hand crushed, clutching against a scarlet thigh, the fingertips bruised, pressing into the flesh of the leg so fiercely that they left indentations. The hand was pierced through, leaving a gaping hole so that stained bones were visible, and, from veins exposed and oozing, blood seeped out the open door. A shard of a face, almost indistinguishable amid the human wreckage. Was it a man? Was it real? Was it alive? This last question had a terrifying answer. Most horrible of all was that watchful, bloodshot eye, fixing me with the vibrant gaze of a living being.

I should not have a stomach to turn sick at such a sight, imagined or truly seen. Have we not watched bull fights in Spain and delighted in the bloody wreckage of the field, whether bull or matador fell? Even so, I tell you that as I stared, appalled, through my mind's eye, upon that hideous, contorted form, the misgiving in my heart turned to horror.

I was ill. I was mad. I turned from the sinister box, rushed back down through the columns, forced my way through the heavy doors, and hurried out into the refreshing coolness of the night. I could breathe again. There was no Magdalen on the steps, but her penetrating gaze bored through my memory, and I ran from it.

You know I find life too pathetic to bother with reckless decadence. A life such as ours takes all the originality out of such encounters, exposing them for what they are—utilitarian animalism, to be had cheaply and valued not at all. But I tell you, I left that horrible place desperate for corporeal relief at its most puerile. I wanted flesh, and I wanted it quickly.

I found the girl on the street, as one does. Down by the Danube. I glanced into the ugly green depths of the river and thought of filth. And then I looked up and saw her. A miserable object, well suited to my purpose. Blonde, with straggling hair and small, dull eyes. Rather like that girl in Vienna. Do you remember her? She wept when we left, but I think it was because she wanted more money.

We haggled over price. She did not seem to be interested in the negotiation, which also suited my sense of economy (which I do have, although you may scoff). I loathe the idea of paying exorbitant sums for such meagre fare.

We wound together through dark, dirty streets. I did not bother to romance her or even to touch her, and she did not seem to expect it.

The place we entered was tedious and familiar, like all those places are. "Do move quickly," I said with impatience. "I shall catch some foul disease if I stay here long."

She could not understand me—her English was limited to the terms of bartering—but she began undressing. A familiar process, easily accomplished.

I watched, with little interest, glancing around the room to survey the filth and squalor, eager to have the thing done and be on my way. And then something caught my eye. There, entwined in the bars of the rickety little bed, was a worn, wooden string of beads. My blood ran cold. The throbbing heartbeat echoed once again in my ears, as if that box were hidden somewhere in the sparse, ugly room.

"Take that out," I said to the girl. "Out of the room."

For the first time, she looked surprised. I thought she had not understood. I repeated myself, gesturing to show the object of my displeasure. I would not touch the thing itself. The girl's filth I could endure as a disagreeable necessity. The taint of contact with that silent irritant I could avoid.

Do not mock me or laugh at this careful reiteration of scene and dialogue. I know that the days of Clarissa are over, but you must be patient with me. Perhaps this retelling will free my mind from the confusion and distress that overwhelm it now.

The girl frowned and seemed to think—or to try to think. I don't believe she really could collect her scattered wits into anything like a coherent thought. Even so, after a time, she came to a conclusion. I stood there, shivering—the place was damp, as I said. The girl, half dressed as she was, crossed her arms and shook her head.

"I want it out!" I snapped. "Now! Throw it away! Out of the room! Into the hall. Into a corner. I don't care. But get it out!"

She reached out for the beads and held them for a moment, considering the scratched, worn baubles in her hand. She shook her head again.

I think I went quite mad then. Who cares for such a wretch? Have we ever felt anything so passionate as hatred for such a worthless object as a prostitute? But in that moment, I wanted very much to kill her. To batter her face into bloody nothingness. To tear that moment into shreds and blind my soul to the memory. To silence the ceaseless throb of that demoniac heart.

I struck her once, hard. She fell in a heap on the ground, groveling, weeping, and clasping those cursed beads to the reddening mark on her face.

I raised my hand to strike again. I would obliterate that mewling cow and rend the primitive necklace into a thousand pieces, scattering its false enchantment and ridding the room of that oppressive feeling.

Then it happened.

I tell you she was as unlike the Magdalen as she could possibly be—slight, blonde, waspish, and stupid. Soulless. Empty. Dead. Yet as I stood there, staring at that trembling, revolting little object, I thought Magdalen Montague stood there before me, more captivating and powerful in this wretched appearance than even my beleaguered memory presents her. Ever and ever, my brain shook with the report of the throbbing heartbeat. I moved away, and the vision shifted. The Magdalen merged with that appalling, bloody mass—that thing crammed into the box in that wretched church. The heartbeat mounted to a deafening pitch.

I felt dizzy. I was ill. I ran from the room and out into the night like a mad animal.

I don't know where I went. I wandered—at least I think I must have. I was delirious, frightened even. Until that moment, I had not known what terror was. Everywhere I went, the Magdalen was there. Everywhere I went, the heartbeat echoed so loudly that my soul shook with each throb.

I thought of death, freedom from this tedious world, escape from the hounding gaze of the Magdalen. Could I find peace—or silence, at least—in annihilation?

I am driveling. And I blot my page like a clumsy schoolboy.

I could not bear nonexistence. To be nothing. To be nowhere. Do you understand? Can you understand? You have always called death a satire. You said a man could fear death or rule it, and you meant to rule it even to the point of deciding when you would die. When you were bored, you said. Bored of the world. But I cannot bear that. And I feared—I still fear—that the thundering heartbeat would have no limits there. In Nowhere it would become absolute.

I cannot kill myself. Fear, as of a child contemplating his mortality for the first time, late at night, all alone—that fear stays my hand.

Perhaps I slept. If so, I dreamed of my father. Or perhaps he was there. But ever, ever, that horrible throbbing.

I awoke in a muddy ditch somewhere in the countryside.

A man came. A farmer. Stolid, brainless fellow. The sort who has no soul to feel nor mind to endure. I tell you, in that moment, I truly envied him his brute peace. He brought me here. Domokos Juhász brought me in and forced me to rest. Or to go through the motions of rest. The ghost of the Montague with the pitiless sound of her God, vengeful in his approach, ceaseless in the throbbing of his heartbeat, has followed me.

Morning has come. It is bright and bustling; discordant and deafening. Like that accursed throbbing in my brain, in my very soul. I cannot sleep. I write like a madman. I made a pretense of composure in my opening, but I cannot maintain it. I know I am exposed to the censorious critique of your mind. Your strength will not comprehend this weakness of mine. I know you of old.

Devil take the mongrel horde. They do not feel. They do not think. Why can they not be silent?

Domokos Juhász sits beside me, quietly watching, his wicked face darkened. What is he thinking? Is he thinking of me? Is he thinking I am mad? I wish I could describe him to you, describe him as he sits there. Watching. Watching.

Devil take the Montague. What has she done to me? Must I go farther to escape her? I don't understand this. What strange power does she have over me?

Perhaps I shall travel. Where shall I go? Anywhere but here. Not back to London. Not to Paris. I could not bear your scornful repulse—and you would scorn me. You could not help it. You are ever true to yourself. It is I who waver.

Shall I burn this? Am I mad? Elsewise the world is mad, and I the tortured sane trapped within it.

Domokos has left me. He has gone out, into the street. There is a man there. One of their priests. They are talking…there…in the street. I think they are speaking of me. What is Domokos saying? They have come in. They are downstairs.

If he comes to gloat over me, I shall not acknowledge him.

Perhaps they will not come. Perhaps they will go to another room.

I hear them in the hall. They are coming to me. Domokos Juhász has brought the priest, and they are approaching my door. I am weeping like a child.

~~I shall~~

I leave Budapest tomorrow.

—J.

III: THE RETURN TO MAGDALEN MONTAGUE

4 AUGUST 1902
L—HOUSE, YORKSHIRE

MY DEAR R.,

I apologize for my tardiness in responding. I have been rather ill.

Marvel once again at my address, dear fellow! After a tedious journey and fitful rest, I am reconciled with my father and drawn back into the suffocating familial bosom. At the moment, the said bosom consists of My Revered Pater (hitherto to be known by the respectful initials M.R.P., like some grandiloquent Latinate abbreviation) and sundry ill-kempt servants. M.R.P. looks upon Domokos, who has followed me home from Budapest like some gargoylean guardian angel, with undisguised suspicion. I could more easily explicate the purpose of the boy's existence on earth than I could provide an adequate explanation for his attendance on me; therefore, I make no explanation at all and laugh at the uproar he causes. The servants are terrified and fascinated by him. The slatternly scullery maid is ever to be seen peering at him around corners and through windows, eager to catch him in the performance of a Satanic rite. The only reward she receives for these efforts is a well-deserved cuff on the ear, courtesy of the vile poisoner who calls herself our cook.

It is a wonder that I found M.R.P. at home given that he spends most of the remaining years of his lonely life—thirty-some-odd years since the death of his wife, an occasion which left him the questionable legacy of my good self—at the club, smoking other men's cigars and blustering against the Catholic Emancipation Act, which, having been passed three years before his birth, he feels it is his special province to condemn in spirited terms. In season and out of season, he avoids the pestilential and sodden ancestral home.

And now, my friend, a question: what should you think if I were to return to the faith of my fathers? Not literally, of course. M.R.P. would consider himself honor-bound to die before submitting to the autocratic tyranny contained in a single Papist blessing and would fight gallantly for the sake of the family escutcheon—which, you may be surprised to learn, is still, despite my better efforts, intact enough to feel threatened by Popish taint. If you could have seen the look upon my revered patriarch's face when I broached the topic!

First he goggled. Then he stared. Soon he glowered. Then he glared. Immediately following this lively display of emotion, he commenced sputtering like a frustrated kettle, his face turned a regal shade, and he swore at me, beginning by consigning everyone and everything to perdition and concluding with a series of expletives beyond even *my* ken. I was confounded everywhere but Rome, unless you reflect on the fact that M.R.P. considers the Vatican and Pandemonium as one and the same. I was repeatedly consigned to the latter, and although, due to my newborn religious fervor, I am reluctant to make such a blasphemous correlation, I welcome you to do so.

"Curse you, boy!" roared M.R.P. so that the books on the shelves rattled about like rocks on the tracks anticipating an approaching train. We were sitting in the library at the time, relaxing in enjoyment of our reconciliation and a fine Madeira. His hand shook so that some of the wine spilled.

"Curse you, boy!" he roared again, as if I had not heard the first half dozen iterations. "What do you say, sir? Eh? What do you mean, sir? Eh? Eh?"

I spoke respectfully but firmly and tried to show in a glance my concern for his health and for the sacrilegious (barbarous!) waste of the Madeira. "I am considering becoming a Catholic, Father."

M.R.P. turned a deeper shade and spluttered out a confused mass of curses, disbelief, and disgust. He cast up before me a rather melodramatic and comprehensive litany of my misdeeds. "It's not yer women I objected to so much. Sort of thing…to be expected. Young men… spending money right and left, disgracing the family. The disgrace! The shame! Harumph! Fraternizing with greasy foreigners who won't eat meat like any healthy Englishman! Sitting around all day…striking attitudes…bunch of poseurs…artists and whores!" He said this last as if I had personally invented that most notorious breed of female. Pointed references to the more infamous episodes of my youth surfaced—the police raid in Soho in ninety-four, the fire in Paris a few years ago when D'Aubigne was killed, and that girl who rather theatrically collapsed and died on the family doorstep, holding in her arms the corpse of the child she insisted was mine. They are buried nearby, you know. The grave is well-tended.

I felt dreadfully sorry for the old man. How painful it must be to lose your son to a socially acceptable ill such as debauchery (at least one can talk about it at the club). What joy to regain him (further source of conversation, if not open triumph, over similarly situated fathers whose sons have not yet recovered from the standard initiatory bout with sin)—only to lose him again to the Scarlet Lady (a brutal shame to any true Englishman and not at all the thing a man wants discussed by the other members)! At the same time, I must confess to a degree of selfish delight. It is not often that one has the opportunity to play a starring role in a gothic melodrama, although I seem to have had my share of such opportunities of late. The horrified father, confronted with the dishonorable conduct of his unfortunate son, reads off a catalogue of transgressions—set to music, high-brow fare for the Alhambra. I was tempted to begin composing the necessary lyrics. Rhyming pairs aplenty came to mind—whores/doors, sin/begin, wine/dine, waste/taste, Rome/tomb, Pope/interlope, and so on, but I restrained my glee and was sincerely deferential. "Father," I said, and had to repeat myself several times before I caught his attention. He was rather enjoying himself too, I think.

"Eh? Eh?"

"Father, I should like your blessing."

There was a moment of silence. "My what?" snorted M.R.P. in astonishment.

"Your blessing, Father."

He growled, but I think he was surprised and perhaps somewhat pleased.

"My blessing. My blessing, eh?" He grunted, doggedly pugnacious. "What would you want it for, sir? You flout my will every way you can! Do you just want the details quite clear so you can flout it in every particular? Eh, sir? Eh?"

"Perhaps so, Father. I know I have been an undutiful son"—an emphatic snort indicated his concurrence with this self-criticism—"and have given you pain"— M.R.P. barely restrained himself from striking a martyr's pose—"but I desire your forgiveness, yet again, and ask for your blessing."

My father sat in silence. When he spoke, his voice was a mixture of acerbity and gruff sarcasm. "I can't do a Popish blessing," he said. "I haven't enough candles in the place, and I don't know any bibble babble spells for the business!" And then he roared with laughter at the joke he thought he had made, clapped me on the back until my brain rattled about in my skull, and repeated his jest at least four dozen times more. Ah, M.R.P.! What a fellow you are! A mere song will not suffice. There really should be a comic opera written about the man. Perhaps the Sullivanless Gilbert could be persuaded to produce one more libretto to grace the Savoy.

My chamber is fast becoming that of a credulous and cluttered devotee. During our journey back to England, even in my weakened and dazed state, I managed to collect many of the necessary accessories. I have candles in abundance, so I might easily lend some to M.R.P. for his "bibble babble spells," crosses, beads, a scapular (which is thoroughly uncomfortable and, as such, makes up for the lack of a hair shirt), several scraps of blessed palms that were given me by a beggar woman in Brussels, and a handful of holy ribbons thrust upon Domokos "for zee seek Eengleesh" by a tall, thin French girl with sympathetic eyes.

Domokos is instructing me in the telling of beads. It is a thoroughly complicated business, saved only by mnemonic repetition. During those rare occasions when I am able to stay awake, I feel gloriously gauche.

Domokos has brought with him a small picture—an icon of the Madonna. I must confess that I do not like this picture. What need have we for pallid pastel virgins when we have such goddesses as Magdalen Montague? That tawdry little image is an aesthetic insult.

But I do not say so to the devoted boy. I would not deprive him of his innocent idolatry.

Now I am being lectured by my Hungarian horror who insists, in broken language too vehement to be misunderstood, that I overtax my strength. The truth of the matter is that I have been chuckling over my own cleverness, and Domokos thinks this private hilarity must be a sign of returning fever.

Therefore, from my harried sickbed, and with the shrewish din of the boy resounding in my ears, I remain,

YRS, ETC.

---

8 AUGUST 1902
L—HOUSE, YORKSHIRE

MY DEAR FELLOW,

Shake your head and look upon me with disapproving scorn, but I must inflict my enthusiasm upon you. I realize that I have not allowed you ample time to respond to my last tender missive, but I must tell you of the latest fascinating experiences of my infant religiosity—vignettes of my encounters with Popery and Papists.

First, I must inscribe upon the page of history the tragic saga of the scullery maid's pious obsession. She followed Domokos about in the most marked manner (as I believe I mentioned in my last letter), succeeding only in catching the attention of every other resident of the house. I have no idea what Domokos thought or thinks of it. Who can know what goes on behind that hideous physiognomy! But she startled me several times by appearing from behind doors and even once scrambled out from under the bed when I returned to my room for an enforced rest. This all concluded a few days ago when she managed to lock herself in the cellar. It seems that she suspected Domokos of hiding carcasses of dead animals in dark corners among the preserves—for ritual sacrifices, I suppose, although I always thought live victims were preferable. She was looking for these tools of the occult—the carcasses, not the preserves—when the door swung to and left her in darkness. The girl screamed herself into a fit and, even though she was confined for a mere half minute while the startled cook fumbled with the lock, it took a great deal of sherry to calm her. Then the cook dealt the scullery maid a resounding box on the ear and sent her back to her mother, taking with her a diverse collection of penny dreadfuls.

Now for my burgeoning religious fervor. The nearest Popish installation is quite small and of recent construction. Of course the larger, more ancient churches nearby bear all the marks of Tudor reclamation. I never thought much of Elizabethan losses except as a sound lesson to tyrannous priests, lecherous monks, and sinister nuns, but the emptiness of that lost, once-hallowed space is poignantly sad—so many churches, once Catholic, stripped by royal edict or destroyed in a mob's frenzy.

But enough of my empathy with suffering long past. I spoke with the priest. He is a thoroughly stupid person in many ways, but one imagines many of the original Twelve were tedious when in company. I really think the tax collector must have been pedantic, Thaddaeus was a nonentity, and we know the multifarious flaws of the Iscariot. What a paradox! Can a man be so unworthy of existence and at the same time celebrate the Divine Sacrifice? He calls me "*monsieur*" and "*signor*"—as if my travels had transformed me into a sort of honorary foreigner.

There is a little old woman who frequents the church—a modern Miss Bates with all the noxious prattling and ingratiating mannerisms guaranteed to drive every sane soul to distraction. Some days when I see her, I understand why Raskolnikov chose an old woman as the target for his Napoleonic hatchet work. Always dithering away about the insufferably dull events in her drab little life, with her silly little ways, and her affectations to intellectualism. They cannot all be Magdalen Montagues, but must they be so primitive? She is forever lighting votive candles. The simple creature looks like a child with her rheumy eyes raised in supplication to the plaster saints.

I must go. I am summoned to dine with my father. Since I first announced my religious interests, M.R.P. has insisted on loading down the table with candles to support me when I "pray a Popish blessing" over the food. I think that he enjoys the contemplation of my "perversion" more than I do.

Yrs, etc.

---

15 August 1902
L—house, Yorkshire

Dear R.,

Again I must anticipate your letter, which I hope will arrive soon? I must tell you of the strange and wonderful experience of this morning. Shall I call it "a memorable fancy?" It is true that I have beheld a world of delights closed to my senses five.

It was early, and I was possessed by that aimless restlessness characteristic of the convalescent. I left the house in the brusque chill of a grey dawn, and wandered about the damp lawn. I passed through neglected gardens (landscape gardening has ever been beyond our income) and trudged through the dew-crested grass, disrupting the lacy film of morning cobwebs, hitherto unspoiled. I was not unhappy, but I was not entirely contented. My peace was not broken, but it was ruffled. I had slept badly and half-remembered dreams or the dim impression of lost memories troubled me. So I walked on.

There is a place in the far corner of the lawn—a cluster of aged trees, where oaks and elms crowd together in the most inartistic manner, closely hemmed in by brush and seemingly impenetrable. It is the sort of place that one generation declares beautiful, and the next condemns as hideous, but which all generations are disinclined to change—not out of affection or any sentiment beyond the dislike of parting with one's money for the sake of rearranging an arboreal scene.

I know the place well. This closely thicketed and secret bower was a favorite haunt of my childhood. There is an entrance hidden among the boughs and bushes—a tight fit but not one beyond the powers of a slender boy nor yet of a slim man made leaner by illness.

A momentary discomfort endured, and I was in the playhouse of my childhood imaginings. My ship, my castle, my prison, my stage, my place of quiet thoughts, exuberant joys, and oppressive sorrows. I sat upon a well-loved rock, leaned against a well-loved tree trunk, and gazed about at the extent of my childish kingdom, my eyes often roving upward toward the silent trees, far hidden from the intruding sky. I was soon lost in fitful remembering.

A voice startled me from daydreams of the past. Not a voice from heaven; not with Old Testament directness, at any rate, nor the voice of my diseased mind. It was the voice of Domokos. At first I thought he was seeking me with all the righteous indignation of a protective nurse and prepared myself for chastisement, but his voice was not angry or full of sickbed concern. It was calm. He pronounced the words with cadenced regularity. He was telling his beads, murmuring the words rhythmically and without undue emphasis, as if they were merely the backdrop of his quiet meditation as he paced the lawn outside my dear nook. Ave Maria…and Ave Maria again.

My beads were in my pocket. I took them out and looked at them. Strange things with the power to stir a man's soul to ecstatic contemplation. I thought of Domokos, not of myself. I sat, staring into the middle distance, listening to the soothing repetition. Ave Maria…and Ave Maria again.

I say I did not sleep. My eyes were wide open, yet I saw nothing of the physical world before me. The bower was lost, transformed into a high, barren, and desolate place. Not desolate. Not barren. There, standing before me in brutal starkness against an angry sky, was a dark, shadowy cross, and upon it a despised, neglected figure gazing down upon me. It was so disfigured it scarcely seemed a human form, yet it was a body—bruised, broken, and bleeding, suspended from unfeeling wood and unrelenting iron. My soul cried out at the sight.

I was not frightened. I did not cringe. I know my Lord and could recognize him. I collapsed into the dust before his bloody glory, yearning to be washed clean, to drown in that blood, to cleanse my unworthiness of the love in his gaze. The effect upon my soul is palpable, even now. This strange, reviled corpse was a wondrous sight in my eyes. I am overwhelmed with love at the very thought of it. A vision of Christ triumphant.

And as I knelt before my Lord, trembling with love in that mighty Presence, I felt the presence of another. A lesser presence but only as all things must be to him. Someone stood behind me. And as with a soaring melody that rises to meet the steady pulse of an already glorious song, the lesser joined with the Greater in an exquisite harmony.

It was the Montague. Whence else could come that palpable strength? That extraordinary personality reverberating in the air? I could sense her magnificent beauty, splendid in the swelling of love as she too gazed upon the crucified Christ. She who had been my hidden guide to that place.

I turned to face her and was amazed.

It was the Virgin. Quiet, unshrinking. Gazing up, like me, upon the spectacle of omnipotent humility. My expectations had been disappointed, yet it somehow seemed as if her presence surpassed that of the imagined

Montague. I looked—with impertinent curiosity, it must be owned—into the eyes of the Virgin. Bright, luminous eyes they were, eyes that might be any color (and have been, under the imaginative brush of the artist for centuries gone by), and a gaze that pierced through the heart into the secret recesses of the naked soul, dispelling the darkness there with an unflinching light, a light to lay all things bare with brutal justice, and to soothe the ache of long-hidden sorrows with the gentle caress of a mother's smile. The Son had eyes like his Mother, but the gaze in her eyes was his.

She looked at me and whispered my name, and my heart, broken long ago and forced away into forgetfulness, became too heavy to bear. I cried out and called her by a name I have never called a living woman and have withheld from the dead woman who, by the laws of science and of family feeling, deserves it. The Virgin took me in her arms and embraced me.

Slowly, gently, the vision passed away, and I was left kneeling, clasping the beads to my lips. Far in the distance—or was it nearby?—I heard Domokos singing the "Salve."

You will scoff at my visions—indeed, I can almost hear you now, canting and crowing in angry disgust. You think me mad, you think me soft, you think me cowardly, you think me addled in my senses. You would have me before you for a mere five minutes that you might talk sense back into me. You imagine the scene and plan the phrases with which you would berate me out of my madness.

This is not madness. The madness was in the delusion that there was ever aught of joy in an orphan's desolation. Despite my vanities, debaucheries, selfishnesses, cruelties, flippancies, and willful rejection, I am embraced. I am the least worthy of such love, but I am beloved. I can only hope and pray that someday you will have share in this most happy wrack.

I shall not begrudge you your fatted calf. I enjoy such a feast, kneeling at my Lord's feet and held in my Mother's arms.

Believe me to be, as ever,

YOUR DEVOTED FRIEND, ETC.

---

14 SEPTEMBER 1902
L—HOUSE, YORKSHIRE

DEAR R.,

I received your letter a fortnight ago. It is just as I expected. I tried to prepare my reply in anticipation—to articulate my defense and give an account of myself, to meet each thrust of your satirical critique with a parry so clever and reasonable that even the fortress of skepticism in which you reside could not withstand the truth. But I know it can make no difference. I struggled long before finding the courage to take up my pen. I shall tell you, but you will not understand. Only if you are taken unawares as I have been, dragged kicking and screaming and thrown off the cliff, down into the precipice, into the void, there to discover that you have been suffocating in the void all along and only now you are truly alive, only now you are able to breathe—only then could you understand.

You have chastised me, denounced my letters as "the narrative of a puerile romance," called me coward, and urged me to return to the "sacred texts" of my apprenticeship in decadence—Pater, Wilde, Swinburne, Baudelaire, Gautier, Rodenbach, Huysmans. I read the novels of Durtal long ago. I did not understand them. How could I, with a mind so shallow and a heart so perverse? I lacked the breadth of vocabulary, the breadth of soul.

You may be outraged and offended by my frankness, seen by you as unfamiliar presumption from your usually docile henchman, but I am moved by the affection I bear you to challenge you thus. There is nothing original or lasting in your determined embrace of rebellion. On the contrary, I fear it does a great deal of harm.

My life until now has been a hollow thing. I tried to fill the aching want, the grasping need, with pleasure. Empty pleasure. How dull and senseless we found it. What drives a man to wallow in dreary despair? Sloth? Or is it evil? True, tangible evil? I have not turned Puritan. On the contrary! My soul, enriched by its encounter with the Divine, moves and delights my body more than tawdry indulgence ever could. Not pleasure. Joy.

It seems that certain moments in one's life are chiefly defined by the irrepressible need a man feels to reorganize his library. A certain branch of my collection—the most colorful branch, from Cleland to Beardsley and beyond—has been destroyed, as have been all the decorative postcards. I knew it must be so. Domokos would not even touch the box in which the pictures were housed. Had he known what sort of books they were, I am sure he would not have gone near those tainted shelves either. You will see this as a sign of weakness and diagnose an early demise to my convictions. It is not so. I have no need or desire for these things. They haunted and hampered my precious peace.

And Magdalen Montague—for you have thrown her up to me as well, although you cloaked it in as many offensive terms as you could concoct. I know any chastisement or defense will seem like hypocrisy on my part. Have I not maligned that lady with my perverse, willful fancies? I will not explicate Magdalen Montague to you. I never could.

Forgive me, my dear friend.

—J.

1 OCTOBER 1902
L—HOUSE, YORKSHIRE

DEAR R.,

You have not understood at all. Of course, you could not.

I was sorry to receive your "*cadeaux.*" Do not attempt to replenish my discarded shame. All like parcels shall be destroyed. I would not quarrel with you, but I shall not turn from this unsought certitude, however much you cast up records of my past infamy. You shall not shame me away from Him. I know too well the full extent of my sin. I am degraded in the dust, worse than a brute animal, for I know what it is that I have done. But I glory in this past—not for what it was, but for its transformation. Shall I cower in mortification and self-pity, turning away from love itself?

How petty are your cheap erotica in the face of this reality.

I shall pray for you.

—J.

11 December 1902
Sackville Street, London
To Mr. R. at Paris.

Dear Sir,

Your letters of 11 October, 25 October, and 16 November 1902, and the package of the fifth inst. having been forwarded to this address from L— house, Yorkshire, are hereby returned to you with the notification that the gentleman to whom they were sent no longer resides at this establishment. We have no forwarding address.

Very respectfully,
John Q. Owens, Esq.

IV: THE DISCIPLE OF MAGDALEN MONTAGUE

11 July 1914
St. Mary's College, S—

Dear R.,

I recently encountered a face from our joint past—a young earl and eager profligate, though not so young as formerly and more inclined to high-minded pomposity. He provided me with your address. Although I remember well your abhorrence of anything resembling sentimentality, I own that I have thought of you often in the passing years. I shall venture into even more objectionable territory when I assert furthermore that I remember you daily in my prayers. I hope you are well and have remained safe in these anxious times

Yrs, etc.

30 August 1914
St. Mary's College, S—

My dear R.,

I rejoice to learn that the years have not dampened your fervency of spirit nor age withered your compositional imagination, particularly in the use of invective. I do fear, however, that your originality is on the wane. Your letter reads rather like an evangelical sermon of a century ago.

I am not "repressed and ashamed" and have not deliberately "concealed" my current abode. I think it is likely that I am a "superstitious fool." I am, in any case, a willing "slave of the Scarlet Lady." Yes, I am at the College of St. Mary's at S— and shall soon graduate from the ranks of "priestcraft" tutelage into full-fledged "Papist villainy." As for MM, you seem to think that all priests and nuns are massed together in a sort of underground network of infamy where I can "finally relieve" that "bizarre passion." I have not seen her, though she is present in my thoughts—just not in the way you imagine.

Despite this shocking revelation, I hope you can accept me to be,

Yrs, etc.

19 September 1914
St. Mary's, S—

Dear R.,

I have attained heights of complicated amazement to rival Mr. Willet the elder! Can it be that curiosity has conquered revulsion? If you meant it in jest, you should have said so, for now I feel licensed to bore you with sundry spurious details of my present life.

I spent some years abroad—years that were as unlike as can be from those long years wasted on the Continent. Time spent in another world. A monastery of Dominican friars took me in. They suffered my moods, soothed my troubles, and guided my wandering interests. They soon disabused me of the delusion that I was master of all things *Catholique*. Several of them have merited sainthood by their resistance to the impulse to throttle "Montague"—for as such was I known, owing to habits of talking out loud in my sleep. I left shriven, baptized, anointed, and full of religious zeal. I have been led here.

As to the "Hungarian horror," Domokos, my faithful acolyte, is with me still. I wonder how many men bring a gargoylian guardian angel with them to the foot of the altar. I could not dismiss him if I wanted to, and I do not want to. He is at home every place where God is most palpably present. Thus, in addition to his other duties, he serves me as a spiritual *Virgula divina*.

He does not bother to improve his English, yet everyone understands him. The townspeople were inclined to distrust him, but he has overcome even the staunchest country prejudices. Even the feelings stimulated by the news we hear from Europe cannot make Domokos anything less than a local favorite. They shower gifts upon him—baskets of fruits, vegetables, meats, small animals, flowers, or whatever they have to hand.

Who can know his feelings regarding the present turmoil consuming his homeland? A letter came for him one day. Perhaps it informed him of death, perhaps it maligned him as a traitor, perhaps it said nothing at all of importance. I could not ask him, and he did not say. I know he has no family of which to speak—none but I.

One day I asked him if he ever yearned to depart from me and commence his own life. He frowned, creasing his eyebrows together for a moment before his face broke into a hideous, glorious smile. Then the fellow laughed right in my face. He left me, shaking his head and still rocking with hilarity. I heard his merry laughter echoing down the hall long after he had gone.

As to my pedantic endeavors, I have learned that Dionysian revels and Paterian self-aggrandizement are not conducive to scholarly prowess. Often when I articulate some lofty thought, supporting the brilliance of that truth with what I consider to be fittingly beautiful language, old Father Jordan smiles and urges, "Lovely… but let us develop strength of understanding before we craft clever, fancy phrases."

Do not think from this that beautiful language is condemned or discouraged. Those few times when I have escaped the habits of eclectic and unintelligible musing to wed language and truth, the priests have applauded my performance. There is nothing more satisfying than capturing a glimpse of truth. Even in Greek.

With regard to my "fellow priestlings," you are quite right. While many of those here are agreeable companions, there is one—the apotheosis of a self-righteous driveller. Avid dislike of him is the familiar staple of my confession. He insists he has been guilty of a dark, sinful past, and imagines between our two selves a sort of camaraderie of reformed profligates and circulates *on dit* too insidious to risk an outcry against open libel. I am forever suffering his hypotheses about the sins I have or have not committed. I do not know whence he has discovered a catalog of my past peccadillos since I avoid confidences with the man as I would hope to avoid the plague.

I came upon him the other day, holding forth on the subject of repented transgressions. It was not an hour for recreation, and I hoped the rector might come upon the fellow and chastise him for speaking without necessity, but human justice is imperfect.

"We reformed men of the world," he declared to the unfortunate young seminarian he had captured as an audience, "do not dwell upon our past sins, yet we must not forget them. We must strengthen each other in the sincerity of our conversions. There is one brother here whom we all know well. He has been the most egregious sinner of them all. Should I, who know the appalling experiences of his youth, hold it against him? No! Shall we condemn the man because of the follies committed in the past? Orgies are nothing! Greed is nothing! Drunkenness, debauchery, and licentious cruelty are nothing! His women! Score upon score of women! It does not matter that he has been the personal lieutenant of Beelzebub! He is forgiven! And every day, the sufferings heaped upon him in this life are nothing. He should be eternally grateful for such discomfort! And he is! I am sure! If he were here..."

I scurried away into the garden so I might not be called upon to give testament. It is not that he is wrong in accusing me of past sins, but this assumption of intimacy offends me deeply. I am thankful that my indiscreet babblings while asleep have not lasted to the present day, for what horrible rumors could the man concoct about the name of MM! I pity the affable yokel who turns to that sensationalist gossip for counsel. Some days I think he was formed by God specifically to try my patience. But instead of setting about his head with whatever piece of furniture is closest to hand, I pray that God grant me more patience and him more discretion. This is the way of my new life—weaknesses are simply the opportunities for poignant requests to the Almighty for his intervention. If I can keep myself from beleaguering the man with chairs, no matter how much the blighter deserves it, and abandon myself to Divine Providence at regular intervals, all manner of things shall be well.

I anticipate your next question: What sort of God would have such an insufferable fellow as his priest? How foolish you are! You have openly invited me to patronizing catechesis! And here is my response: If I did not believe that he can transform even the most irritating of sinners, I could not believe in my own reformation. There. Now I am done with preaching. For now, at least.

You ask how I like this life. I am at peace. I am joyful. At the same time, do not think I frolic along a gently winding path strewn with pale pink rose petals. In fact, I should say that the overwhelming feeling of my present life is exhaustion. With studies, duties, and the pressing needs of the people hereabouts that cannot be thrust into either category, there is no time left. And far too many things are left undone.

Aside from our religious duties, there are many activities to fill our time. Some of our more vigorous members spend every available moment playing cricket. The less energetic dedicate themselves in thespian revels. Last year I played Oedipus with a Jocasta rather inclined to impromptu hilarity during the performance (taken as hysteria appropriate to the character and encouraged). We performed in Greek, of course. Our tastes are chiefly, but not exclusively, classical. Occasionally we take on the Bard himself, and this year we played *The Importance of Being Earnest* to great acclaim. Aside from such frivolity, I spend a great deal of time with Father Thomas, a simple old man and devotee of the sick. I often rise early and assist him in the infirmary.

There are days when my brain is so overcharged with thought and study that I feel incapable of praying. One evening, some weeks ago, I received special permission to remain awake past time and remain in adoration before the monstrance. I knelt down, joyous at the prospect of reorganizing my scattered wits. I woke the next morning curled up across the kneeler, profoundly cramped and frustrated. I had dreamed of Magdalen—Magdalen as my wife and the strange life we would have shared.

I am daily reminded of how much I lack of holiness. I have been reading the autobiography of a little French saint, Thérèse of Lisieux. I wonder if it is sinful to find a saint tedious. I did so at first. You would disdain her entirely. I have been told by Father

Thomas, not unkindly, that I have a streak of ambition that mitigates against humility. He supposes it is because I have read too many French novels.

I must go. Domokos has come to remind me of evening obligations. My prayers are with you always.

Yrs, etc.

---

12 October 1914
St. Mary's, S—

My dear R.,

I am writing to you out of pure selfishness. I hope thus to exorcise restlessness and clear my head, stupid with exhaustion, so that I may sleep.

Domokos is gone. He came to me some days ago and requested permission to return home for a time. I gave it, weeping. He is gone, and I feel strangely alone. Shall he be one of those thousands we hear dead?

But enough of such melodrama.

Word came this evening of old Sally Heaton, a poor woman who lay suffering in extremis. Father Thomas went out to minister to her, and I accompanied him. Father Thomas is an old man, inclined to neglect care of his own aged frailty.

The old woman lived—if it can be said that such a miserable wretch could live—in a dank, smelly hole stagnant with filth and disease. Not even Victorian officiousness could rescue the Heatons. They are of a breed that clings to privation as a personal birthright.

Old and wrinkled like an emaciated monkey, Sally Heaton lay huddled under a pile of faded rags. I have seen rags like those before, worn by prostitutes and cripples alike. There is no moral requirement for abject wretchedness. One need only rot through life and into death. You may think that I am too imaginative or that the immoral caprices of my youth have made too profound an effect on my impressionable mind, and I am determined to put on a sort of perversely apocalyptic philanthropy. But I know that place for what it is.

Sally Heaton's only surviving relative was there, an illegitimate granddaughter. The girl stood, ragged and frightened, huddled against the door, staring in wide-eyed horror at this picture of her own future. What could she expect in life but poverty and wretched death?

It was a ghastly sight. In her racking pain, the old woman looked with bestial desperation toward Father Thomas, who, despite his own age and frailty, moved quickly toward the bed, a graceful picture of benevolent and unselfish concern.

As he bent down, she retched into the air and into his face. Sally coughed as her granddaughter, still frightened, struggled to clear the refuse from the bedclothes.

I stepped forward in shocked concern for the priest, but he rejected my overtures of assistance and wiped his face with a handkerchief. Old Sally grabbed at his arm and whispered, spitting the remnants of vomit as she urged Father Thomas to lean toward her face. Without hesitation, he did.

I moved away until I saw Father Thomas raise his hand in the blessing of absolution, then stepped forward to help where and if I could.

What little blood had been in the face of Old Sally Heaton was gone. Thus shriven, she seemed more shriveled and corpse-like than before. She breathed with rough heaviness, as if the air itself were practicing for a death rattle.

Her body was racked with the pain of an unseen frenzy, and she writhed upon the bed. After a moment, she seemed to settle, but her mind was feverish, and she stared wildly from one to the other of us. Father Thomas moved forward, yet again, to soothe this dreadful anguish.

She flinched, as if frightened of his hand, and as she did, the swift perverseness of fatal illness showed itself. Her eyes had shone with the light of a desperate spiritual hunger. Now they were a picture of irrational and frenzied hatred.

She moved with alacrity disproportionate to her age and sickness, drawing her hand back, then thrusting it forward to strike the priest brutally across his face.

Father Thomas started back from the slap in stunned surprise, then rested into placid pity. I stepped in to protect the old man from her violent delirium but was gently repulsed.

The repressed exhaustion of so many weeks rushed over me in a blind indignation. This poor old man had been summoned like a dog to serve this pathetic old woman, a rotting soul, half-crazed in her old age and delirium. And this was to be the repayment for so holy an old man? Was this how God repaid his loyal servants? The world is collapsing, thousands dying in horrendous agony and without consolation, and this wretch, blessed by the presence of a priest, would strike him? And I thought of you, my friend, and was angry with you for your willful blindness.

These thoughts flashed across my mind in a mere instant…and were just as quickly thrust aside in recognition of what I saw before me—and that was something of Magdalen Montague. Father Thomas raised one hand to his rapidly discoloring cheek but did not take his other hand from her clammy arm. The woman's face changed again.

The earnest hunger reappeared, wedded now to poignant dread. Death was in the room.

Father Thomas began to administer the sacrament.

I cannot describe the reality of the anointing. Divine power, palpably present in all of the sacraments, is most clearly felt in the last of them. It is as if God's ultimate gift in this earthly life, the supernatural grace of final perseverance, were so great that it needs must shake the room.

We stayed with Sally Heaton until she was dead and brought the weeping, frightened child to stay with a charitable farmer and his wife who live nearby.

You might expect that this was the catalyst for an intense religious vision, full of torrid melodrama and mysticism. You might think I would have been catapulted into some extraordinary experience, confronted by the shattering revelation of a spiritual reality. This letter to you would demonstrate my trauma through stuttering ellipses and sentence fragments.

No, nothing of the sort. If my style seems at all deteriorated, it is because I am growing more and more tired as the minutes pass—too tired to be artful. On our return home, the old man was talkative and pleasant, but he spoke mostly of flowers. He is an amateur horticulturist. We saw some mice along the road, and it made me think of Browning.

It was not an extraordinary scene, really. Death is the everyday prerogative of this church. At the moment when humanity is at its most vulnerable, these priests stand like guardians, warding off the fiends who would carry this or that soul to hell. Each victory is itself wondrous.

I do not express myself well.

I shall not think of it now. I shall sleep. Anything I think or write now is sure to be histrionic. For now, believe me to be your very exhausted friend,

—J.

P.S. I was about to seal my missive when I realized I had received your last in my absence from home. I have read it, and it has troubled me deeply. How can you ignore the chaos all around you? You must not think that by burying yourself ever more in corruption, you will escape from the reality of death. You only bring greater desolation upon yourself. I am too weary to scold more. My prayers you cannot escape.

---

25 May 1915
St. Mary's, S—

Dear R.,

I apologize for the time it has taken me to respond to your several letters. I cannot think why you persist in this correspondence. I know the joy it brings me and know likewise how much you despise what I have become.

I am glad to have received the repeated assurance of unruffled, dismissive calm in the face of this tragic unfolding in Europe. Should you not depart from the city—not in admission of denied concern, but as a practical consideration for safety?

Here, the days continue hectically, and exhaustion fails to distract from the horror of thought. Even as the days pass and we draw nearer to that most blessed day, all things are overshadowed by the destruction of Europe. I think of Domokos and pray. Shall I ever know what has become of him? I think too of dear Magdalen and pray.

I shall depart soon, but for what place? We green recruits evince all the reckless eagerness of our sort. We all want to be doing something very intense and dangerous indeed. We would be caring for the sick, but only those with deadly and contagious diseases. We would be missionaries serving wherever persecution is most fierce, and we are assured of violent and dramatic martyrdom. We would travel to the farthest reaches of the Empire and convert savages, preferably cannibals. We would be at the Front, ministering in the midst of hell. We would be doing *something*. We cannot stand by in silence while the world obliterates itself.

Word comes daily, but the news is so belated that thousands more may have died in the interim. A new terror has been unleashed beyond the wildest of nightmares. One fellow here insists this is the end of time—but there is no time to speculate. What man, woman, or child, can be helped by it? Thousands and thousands are dying. The world is drowning in a sea of suffering. Shall there ever be peace again? Can Ypres ever be forgotten? What will the world be like when this horror stops? Will it stop?

I pray for you constantly, my friend.

—J.

---

22 June 1915
St. Mary's, S—

My dear R.,

It is done. I heard no voices and saw no visions.

Last night I prayed long in the chapel, like a knight holding vigil, preparing and purifying before battle. My weaknesses were heavy upon me, and I was haunted by the past. I thrust all thought of past sins away. Even at this late hour, my mind could not articulate prayer. It needed not.

My father was in attendance at the ordination. He spends a great deal of his time in London now—an aged secondary politician, making feeble attempts to stop the onslaught of a world collapse.

He must have decided that an expression of bemused indulgence was most suited to the sacramental occasion. He brought me a gift too—a box of decorative and thoroughly impractical candles for my "bibble babble spells." I know that my father wept when I stepped forward and the bishop's hands were laid upon me. He always clears his throat when in denial of such emotions. That noise accompanied my mother from the church to the graveyard. His gruff "Hrumph!" sounded loudly and frequently through the nave again today.

Another figure entered late and stood in reverent silence at the back, like a vagrant awaiting permission before entering this sacred house. His ugly face was aged and tired but unchanged. It was one of the most beautiful faces I shall ever see. I do not know where he has been or what he has seen. Has he searched in vain for a lost family? Is he an escaped prisoner? What carnage has he witnessed? I cannot tell. I know that Domokos could see hell itself yet retain the unshakeable outward serenity of an authentic interior peace. I am full of aching gratitude for his restoration, knowing full well that there are few so restored in the present conflict.

I am not my own. There comes a time when self-abandonment so overwhelms you that you cannot articulate or express it in any way other than through the most theatrical body language. Thus, I lay prostrate with my fellows before the sanctuary. In that posture of transcendent self-sacrifice, we were swallowed up into the mere shadow of our crucified Lord. Such were the words of the bishop.

These hands are no longer mine. When Domokos knelt before me and begged a priest's blessing, I felt smaller and more gloriously insignificant than the most pitiful of beings yet profoundly significant, for I am His priest.

But what of MM? Nothing? Have I forgotten her in the thrill of my new life? No, for now she is my dear sister. She too was with me on that cold, worn floor, with its wooden planks of once-vibrant color drummed into dun-colored familiarity by the tread of eager feet. She is with me now. Dreams of another life are nothing now. Even so far away, she must always remain close to me. Shall I ever see her again? One day, I shall.

The orders are given and we are sent forth. One man goes to the Front, and it is not I. No martyr's crown shall be mine. He shall go and minister in memory of a brother killed in the wasteland of Ypres. The rest of us shall scatter across this cherished island, commissioned to win back what once was lost. This Catholic island.

Domokos and I shall retire to the small village of M— in damp Devon. If I drown, I shall do so with pious enthusiasm. Shall we retreat from the horror that has overshadowed the rest of the world? No. Like the rest, we shall wait, and watch, and pray. I must comfort those left behind and cherish this empty world until our loved ones return. What is the world that is our legacy? Can it be the brave new world we were promised?

I beg God to teach me how to serve him in this time of crisis. I cannot lie and assure those who mourn that all shall be well. I cannot assume an insouciance I do not feel. I can only assure them of the certainty of things to come.

I met a talented young man in London some years ago. You will not know his name. His was a talent destined for future reverence, not the hollow din of a prodigy's triumph. He sent sonnets composed on the battlefield to a friend, and that friend has passed them on to me. It is his words that resonate with me now, and I pray God to keep us all safe:

Safe though all safety's lost; safe where men fall;
And if these poor limbs die, safest of all.

He died but a few weeks ago.

My new home shall not bar me from plaguing you with sanctimonious epistles. I shall continue to pester you with such unwarranted encouragement in the hope that someday you will become so exasperated with my pestering that you will accept God simply to silence me. And when he has you, he shall not let you go. Till then, may he protect you and keep you from harm.

Your devoted friend and
His obedient servant,

—J.

V: THE TRIUMPH OF MAGDALEN MONTAGUE

19 February 1923
M—, Devon

My dear R.,

I have just returned from explaining to an affable, dunderheaded farmhand that chivalry demands he make an honest woman of the butcher's daughter he seduced a few months ago. It was easier to talk sense into his cloddish brain than it ever will be to convince you of anything, my friend. Don't forget that even Swinburne faced death in his time. You cannot hope to escape the inevitable through sheer quantity of sin.

Thank you for the volume of poetry. I have enjoyed it much more than the Mirabeau you sent before. I enclose a copy of *Horace Blake,* which I hope you will read.

The rains continue. During my daily walks, I am bathed in good, honest English mud. This puts me in mind of Proverbs, book the twenty-fifth, verse the twenty-sixth. Perhaps a neighbor can provide you with a Bible so you might investigate the above allusion.

YRS. AFFECTLY, ETC.

---

28 SEPTEMBER 1927
M—, DEVON

DEAR R.,

If such a thing can be possible, I am shocked and appalled by this latest indication of your confirmed profligacy. I do not care who or what has encouraged you to this step. You are a stubborn old fool. Do not expose your ignorance and prejudice by publishing this work! I recognize the time and effort that has gone into the manuscript, but I beg you not to make public this offense against God and his Church! There is a legion of revolting novels available to the public at present. They shall not feel the loss of this single one, but your soul might reflect the omission to its advantage.

Do not bring this shame upon the Church you malign and upon yourself as an obstinate and pigheaded antagonist of the truth.

YRS, ETC.

17 March 1934
M—, Devon

My dear R.,

Poetry is reborn in Devonshire! A collection of ill-kempt young men with artistic aspirations and unsound notions of personal hygiene have deposited themselves in our tiny village. Their purpose is loosely based upon an experiential philosophy, without the beauty of the Paterian paradigm—by associating with the mentally negligible (our good country selves) and bringing the earthiness of ignorance (again, ourselves), they intend to dethrone the classical rigors of prosody. Their "research" principally involves unseemly "orgies" in the fields, which frightens the livestock and angers the farmers; unimpressive attempts at seduction of the local maidens, who are thankfully more inclined to their usual rustic profligacy; and loud fracas in the churchyard at night, when the orgies have failed to satisfy.

Domokos is kind to them, as he is to everyone. Even with my own past, I have little patience for these selfish wastrels. They know nothing of the world beyond their own petty, self-important transgressions. You, I know, would think them the flower of future glories. I think them rather tawdry representations of

Satan's legions more in need of stern parental discipline than of bell, book, and candle. Why must children be so willful and foolish?

I was sorry to hear of your illness. Perhaps a stay at the seaside? As always, I recommend a regular dose of conversion to amend all ills.

YRS. AFFECTLY, ETC.

---

7 JUNE 1940
M—, DEVON

DEAR R.,

Your letter of concern touched me deeply. We are not at the epicenter of chaos, but we do feel the effect of it all. We all wait to learn of new horrors unleashed, especially those of us old enough to remember the legacy of Flanders Field with tragic vividness. A woman of the parish, long aged by the extreme rigors of sacrifice, lost her husband and brother in that Great War. She has now lost a son in what may be a greater one. Familiarity with death has reached new heights in our present era.

Yesterday there was a funeral Mass for a stillborn child. The mother nearly died three days ago in giving birth to her dead daughter, but she stood beside the little coffin today, possessed of a frail and desperate calm of exhaustion too poignant for grieving. After the child was buried, I persuaded the mother to sit, to weep, and then to sleep.

Domokos is the archetypal example of war-time volunteerism. We need no posters in M—. Simply look to Domokos and you will know what you can be doing in the service of your country. He helps enforce blackout regulations, he trains aircraft spotters, he supports the local constabulary, he assists in the development of evacuation plans, and he is a vital (though silent) part of our village security commission. He has disciplined and organized the local children too young to serve otherwise. We are ever driving—we have a scrap drive, a tin drive, a paper drive, a rubber drive—and when we are not driving, we are gardening. I made the mistake of being rather successful in the harvesting of turnips. My turnips were praised countywide until we all became quite sick of their constant appearance for meals: turnip pies, turnip soups, turnip sandwiches, turnip bread. Many of the children have come to consider turnips as a sort of penance inflicted upon them for the sake of their country and the world at large. The young girls, and some of the boys as well, have learned to knit, and cheerfully produce socks and caps of every imaginable size. They can readily serve either significantly overweight or dangerously emaciated men. The latter are, of course, what we expect. Domokos has also joined the LDV and drills with his regiment when he is not drilling with the children.

This is the war as we see it. And each day is overshadowed by the news we hear or do not hear from the Front.

I am summoned to discipline three young children who have absconded with rations beyond their allotment. You will not be surprised to learn that the rations in question were not in any way, shape, or form, turnips.

God bless you and protect you from every evil.

YRS. AFFECTLY, ETC.

---

22 JUNE 1940
M—, DEVON

DEAR R.,

How can you live in the world today and not believe in the tangible reality of evil? How can you stand aside as thousands are ruthlessly slaughtered and oppressed? Have you not heard the cries of Reynaud? Do you not know the dangers of frightened appeasement?

Do you think such fervor unbecoming in a man of the cloth? As ever, you utterly fail to understand. We fight to defend the soul of humanity. The battle is not glorious. It never is. But the selfless service and willing sacrifice of honorable men for the sake of *right*—that is glorious indeed. We fight for the preservation of life, for the protection and reverencing of human dignity, and for freedom.

If I cannot persuade you, the rain of destruction about your head surely must. *Leave Paris!* Depart from Montmartre! You prove nothing by remaining there. And you cannot imagine that you will be spared. Are you blind to the German advances? Brave souls remain to defend and protect, moved to sacrifice out of love. Shall you remain out of perverse and obstinate lethargy? If nothing else moves you, be selfish! Depart for your own safety!

YRS, WITH *GREAT CONCERN* AND AFFECTION, ETC.

---

4 MAY 1941
LONDON

MY DEAR R.,

I can hear your groans over the length of this missive. You open the letter and exclaim with an expletive or two or twenty that you are unjustly burdened with such tomes. What have you done, you may ask, to deserve such affliction? Perhaps you shall turn hypocrite and remind me it is wartime and that we must conserve resources. By all means, you shall say, refrain from composing a dreary epistle, in length comparable to the most tedious of three-volume novels.

Do not chide me. Something has happened to justify a letter of such length—so that even you may consider this indulgence justified!

I am in London. A fellow of mine, ordained at the same time as I, has been killed in the Blitz. He was an old man, though younger than I, and died in the darkness one night when he had left his home to care for the sick. Resources of all kinds are scarce across England, so it would not be easy to replace a deceased priest. I volunteered to take my friend's place in the interim.

There is a young priest assigned to me in Devon, and he has remained to minister to our flock. He was quite determined to venture forth and champion God in the midst of the bombs. I know that reckless enthusiasm all too well, though it would require an extraordinary stretch of the imagination for my young protégée to believe that. But now that I can recognize the wisdom of my own fathers in restraining the headlong rashness of a fresh recruit, I exercise powers of restraint over this young lad for as long as that is possible. Such young men shall be needed all too soon, hungered for by suffering thousands.

But I ramble. I am in London, as I said, serving in a friend's stead.

Some nights ago a young messenger came in the night to summon me with eager invocations to attend at the bedside of a dying nun at Tyburn Convent.

And now I hear more objections from you. I know well your extreme hatred of death stories. For years I have read your complaints and objections. My letters, you insist, drip with deathbed descriptions. Nothing is so macabre, you cry, than the morbid tales I tell! I urge you to strive for patience yet again.

The bombing had ceased rather early that night, and I had been asleep for an hour, but no more. Domokos unwillingly roused me from my bed. I was tired and impatient for my own rest, but I shook myself awake, collected the accoutrements of my office, and ventured out with him, hurrying across the city. Domokos remained behind, patiently watchful beside a low fire.

It was a long walk and often puzzling in the unremitting darkness. Many of the streets have been closed by the Luftwaffe. The young man knew the city well, so we threaded our way through back alleys as rats weave through the sewer, possessed with a sort of second sight and guided by the inner promptings of an unseen instinct.

We were stopped twice, each time by gruff men with watchful eyes and faces strained by night upon night of such lonely watches. London is full of such faces—soldiers, nurses, politicians, and refugees. There are no other classes of people in this changed world.

The city is pervaded by an unearthly quiet. The darkness, sometimes interrupted by the pale beam of regulated and downcast lights, impresses upon each building the aura of grim expectancy. Even the starlight has turned menacing, as it may expose the cloaked security of the besieged city. Each step echoes with horrible resonance in the pregnant silence. The streets are haunted by the ghosts that will be tomorrow. The heaviness of fear intensifies as the minutes pass into hours of darkness. London stands, most vulnerable in sleep, most watchful of cities in the nighttime of war.

Though it felt as if hours had passed since our departure, it was yet three o'clock when we arrived at the convent at Tyburn. You will denounce me as a sentimentalist, but the darkened windows glowed with a serene light. We were received with gracious but obvious haste and taken down gently lit hallways to the cell of the dying nun.

The lights were dim, a condition suited to that simple chamber. Untheatrical asceticism had joined with austere cleanliness to form the room. The preoccupation with knickknacks (so characteristic of a past era) held no sway. There was the bed, a small table beside the bed, and at the center foreground of the wall a large crucifix carved from wood and painted with vivid and colorful detail. The corpus glistened with blood and was twisted unnaturally in the torment of pain, but the face wore an expression of gentle, patient love, transforming the picture of anguish into a vision of ecstatic joy. The room's atmosphere was not sterile; it was rich with the ambiance of presence. I knew it as the presence of Divine Love, radiating from the crucifix and hovering about our heads. I knew another presence too—that of the distinct personality emanating from the bedridden figure of the dying woman herself.

The nun was old and weathered, but her eyes were yet bright. They shone with a deep black lustre that belied her dying mien. *Les yeux sont le miroir de l'âme*—you see that a lifetime of training will not bring the Latin as readily to my lips as its French counterpart. *Oculus animi index*, then. Her hair, once a pure rich black, was streaked with white and peeked out from beneath the veil. She had taken, I was told, the name of an old English saint.

Graceful, silent nuns clustered around the room, stepping back from the bed only to admit the doctor or myself. Many of the novices were there, frightened and young, with eyes brimming over with tears. She had been Mother General, and, though she had set aside such honors when illness made such humble self-abeyance possible, they still spoke of her as such, whispering, "God's mercy upon you, dear Mother."

I leaned over her, and those keen eyes turned toward me. A few moments later, she was shriven and anointed. I opened the pix, and the nuns fell to their knees.

Some time later, with grace still heavy in the room, I exchanged quiet words with the old nun.

"Thank you, Father," she said as I wound up the stole. "I am sorry to summon you from your home at such an unseemly hour. Such a journey is uncomfortable at the best of times and particularly dangerous now."

I smiled acknowledgment of her thanks but did not respond. I have not yet discovered the words with which to respond to such gratitude. It is all too easy to sound disingenuous or arrogant.

"You do not usually serve in London?"

"No. I have come as a temporary replacement for a friend who died some weeks ago. My own parish is in Devon."

"And how do you like Devon?"

"Very well."

"Indeed?"

"Yes. Many years ago, I may have thought that a prolonged sojourn at a country church would be the epitome of dullness, but really, I am fond of it."

There was a brief pause, perhaps owing to pain. "Do you ever miss London?"

"Rarely."

The doctor, a small, energetic man with popping black eyes and an inability to stand still beyond half a second, appeared in the door. "Well!" He conveyed more of a desire to dispel the peaceful reverence maintained in the room than any purpose of articulation. "Well!" he repeated and moved toward the bed. The sisters moved out of his way in a gracious gesture that served them well. He likely would have tramped upon them had they not moved from his path.

He stood over the sickbed, his back turned to the crucifix. Throughout his visit, he cast many uneasy glances over his shoulder, all of which focused upon any part of the wall behind him where the crucifix was *not.*

"Well," was repeated for the third time, but with a change of intonation that boded well for those in the mood for further elucidation. "Well, you look...yes, yes, indeed."

This last, which was in response to nothing whatsoever, was punctuated with several rapid glances over his shoulder. As if to justify this exertion, he caught me in the final returning glance. "Ah, yes. Padre. Visitors are a bit...You should be careful not to tire yourself."

"I sent for him," said the dying nun.

"Indeed? Well, well."

The woman was quietly firm. "I should like Father to remain for some time more, if...if that is possible?"

I bowed my head in response to the note of questioning introduced into the final phrase.

The doctor mumbled something unintelligible, and we stood in silence for some few minutes.

"You have many patients in London these days," I said in an inviting tone.

His response was more of a growl than a mumble, consigning all Germans to hell. He glared at me. "I read somewhere," he announced, "that the whole thing is a Jesuitical plot."

"Oh really?" This sudden change of topic bewildered me.

"Really!"

From this promising beginning, he launched into a full explication of his belief that religion lies at the heart of all evil. He did not go so far as to attribute all the death and destruction of our present age to the machinations of demon Popery (along with the Spanish Inquisition, the Gunpowder Plot, and the common cold), but he did intimate that the Holy Father should be held personally responsible for every poor wretch killed in the bombings. For good measure, he threw in a malicious comment about the insidiousness of the Hebrew. It seems he has come across a copy of *The Protocols* and swallowed that sinister hoax whole. How on earth the Third Reich can manage the thing with the Holy See and the Jewish nation, all the while maintaining a convincing superficial display of hatred, he did not explain. Overall, for a man of science, the doctor spoke an alarming degree of nonsense.

It grows dark and Domokos potters in to beleaguer me on behalf of blackout restrictions and with his concerns for my health.

An unsystematized and wandering mind has ever been my downfall, and age has only helped the fault to flourish. I shall endeavour to focus or else I shall be here at my desk until dawn. Such unnecessary expenditure of strength and electricity would be reckless and irresponsible in one so old and at such a time of national suffering (or so I can hear my own doctor chiding me).

The nun did not die that night, and I returned to minister to her many times in the days that followed.

Yesterday morning I went to see her for the last time. I had not intended to venture forth in the heavy dimness of a murky sunrise. In fact, when I lay down to sleep the night before, I had hoped for sound sleep, unbothered by any interruptions "Jerry" might have planned. I had not slept long—if I slept at all—before the bombs fell. They thundered across the city and came with special violence about our ears. Six people were killed in the neighborhood that night. The bombs came in the midst of a light fog—not of the prestigious pea-soup variety but gloomy enough to introduce a ghostliness into the already haunting atmosphere.

Can you know the full horror of this Blitz? A hail of fire rains down, shocking the darkened city with a sudden blaze of light and maelstrom of noise and terror. In the fog, unseen death comes screeching from the skies, breaking through the cloud of blindness only in the same moment as it makes devastating impact. The air fills with the severed beams of splintering houses. A door here. Roof shingles there. A bicycle. A bookcase with the charred remains of its contents. Whole walls, or a piano, or a sleeping victim all collapse into each other in the torrent of a flaming avalanche. Pandemonium almost buries the sound of screams—almost but not quite. From the flames and turmoil that remain, bodies are removed. Mangled corpses, men reduced to fiery debris. Amid the carnage, tired but resolute men step. They laugh, soothe, and encourage, though their stomachs turn and their hearts grow cold at the sight of such butchery.

I anointed a man whose face was half gone and held in my arms a weeping, crippled child whose mother was spread across the wreckage of her house in a shower of sundered flesh. The child's arm was broken when a window fell in upon his sleeping head.

The faint light of a still-dim morning had come when I, tired, filthy, and stained with the blood of the dead and the dying, made my way home. Too tired to wash and too tired to sleep, I knelt in the church for long hours, waiting for God to teach me anew how to pray. When consolation came, I was not urged to sleep. I was reminded that I was yet needed.

I rose, returned to the house to cleanse death from me so that I might return to battle it with fresh armor, and went through the early morning to Tyburn Convent.

One of the novices came to meet me. Her face, which bore the signs of recent tears, was shining. We passed through darkened corridors—familiar yet different, as if the walls themselves had donned new robes of mourning, as if the horror possessing the city made every brick, every drop of paint, quietly, ceaselessly watchful. This was not the attentiveness of anxiety. These stones have seen more dreadful sufferings than this. Have they not witnessed the fall of man? Rome collapsing about the ears of an aged monk and his lion? The desolation of this present age? The unwavering eyes of the Mother, gazing upon the victorious ignominy of her Son. Ever watchful. Ever watching. And waiting.

My mind grows fantastical, and I lose the thread of my narrative.

The novice led me to the bed of her suffering sister.

The room was dimly lit, as ever. This, at least, was unchanged and unchanging. The peaceful, unfolding drama of this room was unmoved by fanfare or battery. It was God's room, and soon he would take possession of it.

The dying woman no longer appeared in pain. Her face had acquired that unearthly softness so often seen in a dying face—the look of resolute calm and perfect peace.

"Good evening...Father. Thank you...for coming...again."

"How are you this evening?"

"Very well, Father...But...perhaps...I think I shall rest soon." She smiled. "It has been well to see you again," she whispered with an effort.

I agreed, smiling.

"And I shall see you yet again." There was quiet satisfaction in her voice, and the smile did not fade from her face as she looked past me to gaze upon the wooden crucifix. The moments passed. The nun grew still. His arms, held out in welcome, drew her in like a child. We watched in silence as she passed into the eternal embrace with the smile still living upon her lips.

There were no desperate last words. A quiet going. So quiet that we could not have known the exact moment of death.

The doctor hurried into the room at this late moment and stepped forward to examine the patient. He looked upon her with a clinical brusqueness. Then he stopped, frozen in startled contemplation of her radiant face. He stepped back from the bed and looked at me in silence, as if my face were a safer sight than hers. I turned my head to smile upon the crucified Lord. The doctor turned too. His gaze was that of a puzzled child stirred by strange, unknown feelings.

The little nuns clustered about the bed and began to sing "*De profundus*" as I blessed the body of the departed, the doctor standing by, silent and watchful. Sometime later I returned home to Domokos. We prayed together in the church—prayers unlike those desperate, hurried pleas besieging heaven from every corner of the suffering city, prayers of hopeful love.

Magdalen Montague is dead. Magdalen Montague lives forever.

The sirens are sounding.

God bless you, my friend.

—J.

EPILOGUE

On 9 August, 1941, a man died at Natzweiler-Struthof. This was not an abnormal occurrence; many men died in the *Konzentrationslager*. This man died at his own hand.

He was an old man with a ravaged face, yellowing skin, and small, angry eyes. He had not been long at Natzweiler-Struthof, and he had spoken little to anyone. It was not a place conducive to conversation.

The man had lain awake in his bunk in the early morning, staring into the unpromising, dull light of dawn and planning his own death.

Seven men had arrived the day before. *Front National de la Résistance*. They were shot upon arrival. He wondered why the soldiers wasted the time in bringing them to the camp. Why not kill them and leave them beside the road? Leave them where carrion would feast on them. They were only fodder for the furnace here.

He had seen so many men die and felt nothing at their tortured passing—nothing more than relief that he had been spared and terror of what tomorrow might bring.

A fortnight before, a man had died of hunger. He did not know the man's name, but he had been overwhelmed with feeling at his death—envy at his release.

He was old and weak. Why would they prey on him?

He was a man of fierce, unsavory passions, but exhaustion and despair had bled the life from these fleshly distractions. He wanted nothing but death.

Letters sometimes came to the Konzentrationslager. None came for him. How could they, when no one could know where he was? No one could know. No one did know.

He wrote a letter. And sent it.

He would die that morning. He would take his own life, come what may.

He was sent to the quarry with other men. Jews and gypsies mostly, and a little Polish priest who looked confused and bewildered in the midst of this unending nightmare. People like him, although perhaps none as—

He did not regret it. He would not regret it.

The old man did not wait. It only took a moment while the nearest guard had turned away to chastise a poor, shriveled skeleton of a man who did not move as quickly as he had been bidden. The old man climbed up some way and stood among the rocks for a moment, staring down at the dull earth. Then he threw himself into the quarry with the violence of hate, so that his brain would be dashed against the rocks and he might find relief in dark nothingness. Down...down...Ever downward he fell, with arms outstretched in an ultimate act of blasphemy—a symbol of despair so crude as to render horror grotesque.

He did not die immediately. The sound of angry cries—the cries of guards robbed of their prey—sang in his ears. The old man lay among the rocks, blood filling his eyes, a twisted, gory heap of flesh at the feet of the little Polish priest.

The priest did not speak. If he had, it would have made little difference, for the dying man would not have understood. But the priest no longer looked bewildered. He looked into the eyes of the dying man and reached toward him to administer the blessing.

The old man with the ravaged face would have drawn back in horror but could only stare in bloody immobility at the dark little priest.

The priest gazed unwaveringly, and the blessing was given before the butts of vengeful rifles fell on his anointed head.

No word was spoken, but a single tear fell from the old man's unseeing eyes.

The little priest saw it.

Another saw it.

And the final breath that came from those cold lips released the soul of a redeemed man.

FINIS.

ABOUT THE AUTHOR

In addition to her scholarly pursuits, Eleanor Bourg Nicholson occasionally strays into fiction, including her novels *A Bloody Habit* (Ignatius Press, 2018) and *Brother Wolf* (Chrism Press, 2021). A former assistant executive editor for *Dappled Things*, she is assistant editor for the *Saint Austin Review* (StAR), as well as the editor of several Ignatius Critical Editions of the classics. Her work has appeared in the *National Catholic Register* and *Touchstone*, as well as with *First Things* and *The Catholic Thing.*

By day, Eleanor is the Director of Religious Education at St. Thomas Aquinas University Parish, serving the University of Virginia (her alma mater), and, with her husband, homeschools their five children. By night, she reads the Victorians, writes Gothic novels, and cares for toddlers. Visit her at eleanorbourgnicholson.com.

More from Eleanor Bourg Nicholson

Brother Wolf

For Athene Howard, the only child of renowned cultural anthropologist Charles Howard, life is an unexciting, disillusioned academic project. When she encounters a clairvoyant Dominican postulant, a stern nun, and a recusant English nobleman embarked on a quest for a feral Franciscan werewolf, the strange new world of enchantment and horror intoxicates and delights her—even as it brings to light her father's complex past and his long-dormant relationship with the Church of Rome. Can Athene and her newfound compatriots battle against the ruthless forces of darkness which howl for the overthrow of civilization and the devouring of so many wounded souls?

In this sister novel to *A Bloody Habit* (Ignatius Press, 2018), Nicholson explores fatherhood, spiritual authority, the occult, the advent of Modernism in the early years of the twentieth century, and the deep desire for meaning in the heart of a charming neo-pagan heroine.

Brother Wolf

Chrism Press, September 2021

www.ingramcontent.com/pod-product-compliance
Lightning Source LLC
Chambersburg PA
CBHW011436170626
46808CB00010B/3183

* 9 7 8 1 9 4 1 7 2 0 5 0 9 *